P9-DFA-927

BOOK #3

OTTO UNDERCOVER

★ WATER BALLOON DOOM ★

RHEA PERLMAN

ILLUSTRATED BY

DAN SANTAT

KATHERINE TEGEN BOOKS
An Imprint of HarperCollins Publishers

Boca Raton Public Library, Boca Raton, FL

For Beautiful Bella
and Rockin' Roman

Thanks to these guys . . . all the kids in Ms. Simmerman's fourth-grade class at the Aragon School in Los Angeles, Frey (My Bud) Arvanites, and George (Science Czar) Schmiedeshoff.

Otto Undercover #3: Water Balloon Doom

Text copyright © 2006 by Rhea Perlman

Illustrations copyright © 2006 by Dan Santat

All rights reserved. Printed in the United States of America. No part of this book may be used or reproduced in any manner whatsoever without written permission except in the case of brief quotations embodied in critical articles and reviews. For information address HarperCollins Children's Books, a division of HarperCollins Publishers, 1350 Avenue of the Americas, New York, NY 10019.

www.harperchildrens.com

Library of Congress Cataloging-in-Publication Data is available.

ISBN-10: 0-06-075499-0 (pbk. bdg.)—ISBN-13: 978-0-06-075499-0 (pbk. bdg.)

ISBN-10: 0-06-075500-8 (trade bdg.)—ISBN-13: 978-0-06-075500-3 (trade bdg.)

1 2 3 4 5 6 7 8 9 10

First Edition

CONTENTS

Stuff You Can Skip

If you read Book One and Book Two, you can skip all the chapters before the P.S. to the Introduction because you know that stuff already.

Or you might want to read it again because you think those are the greatest chapters ever written.

Or you can just throw this book in the garbage right now, because you hate it already and it's not going to get any better.

Word Puzzle Alert!!!

Look out for words in thick dark letters!

Some of these are backward words.

For example, *retirw* is backward for *writer*.

Some are anagrams. These are words that become other words when their letters are all scrambled up.

For example, *sword* is an anagram for *words*, and *red ear* is an anagram for *reader*.

Keep your *eye* out for palindromes, which are words that are spelled exactly the same backward and forward, like *boob*.

If you think the *retirw* is a *boob* for

making the *red ears* waste their time fig-
uring out word puzzles all day long, don't
worry, you don't actually have to do them.

The answers are on the sides of the
pages.

P.S. TO THE OTHER PREVIEW TO THE INTRODUCTION

Otto Asks a Question

"Hey, you want to hear this song?" asked Otto.

"No," said everyone.

He sang it anyway.

The Song Otto Sang

(In the note of G, with great guitar strumming)

Otto
By Otto

My name is Ot - to, it's al - so Pil - lip

I drive a race-car I built my - self

I named him Race-car be - cause he is one

And 'cause *Del - bert* sound - ed dumb

And 'cause **Race - car** spells **race-car** back - ward

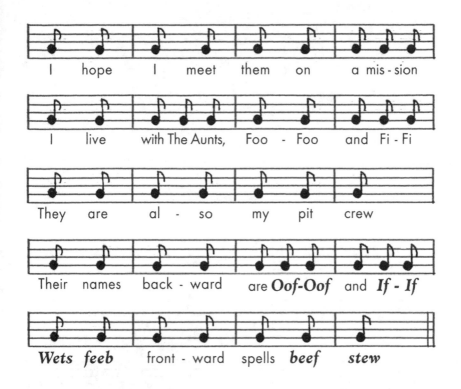

I hope I meet them on a mis - sion

I live with The Aunts, Foo - Foo and Fi - Fi

They are al - so my pit crew

Their names back - ward are **Oof-Oof** and **If - If**

Wets feeb front - ward spells **beef stew**

Bonus Stanza

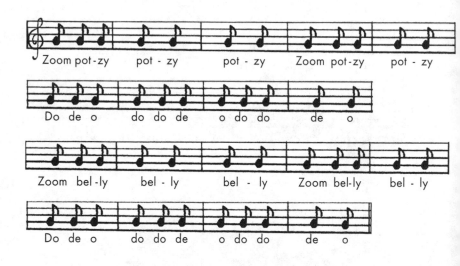

Zoom pot-zy pot-zy pot-zy Zoom pot-zy pot-zy

Do de o do do de o do do de o

Zoom bel-ly bel-ly bel-ly Zoom bel-ly bel-ly

Do de o do do de o do do de o

We interrupt this bonus stanza to bring you
THE STORY

CHAPTER 1

The Fleabag 500

Otto was behind the wheel, in starting position for the Fleabag 500. The race was named after the stadium owner's dog, who was in the book of *Guinness World Records* for continually scratching himself every second for the last 14 years.

Otto's lucky guitar was on the seat next to him.

The despicable Wilson Carlson Fullsom was in position right beside Otto, in car 56.

"Hey **Pullup**, swell banjo," he said. "Let me get a look at it."

"Sure," said Otto. That was the nicest thing Fullsom had ever said to him, even if he did get a few facts wrong, like his name, but at least he had used a palindrome.

Pullup is a palindrome.

Otto held up the guitar.

"It's a guitar," said Otto.

Fullsom had a raw egg. He threw it. Luckily, Otto had enclosed the guitar in a superhard clear, elastic case. Things just bounced off of it. The egg boomeranged back, smashed on Fullsom's helmet, and ran down his face.

Just then an airplane looped across the sky, leaving a trail of sky writing. It said *A*

Clifford Won. Otto always kept his *eye* out for his next assignment. He knew there was no one named A Clifford in the race. This was an anagrammed message for him. He had to go.

"Catch you next time, Foulsome," said Otto. "Car trouble." He pulled a lever, and *smoke* poured out from a *smoke machine* under Racecar's hood. Otto disqualified himself and left the track.

Wilson Carlson Fullsom couldn't believe his luck. Without Racecar in the race, he had a pretty good chance of winning.

He got out of his car and started yelling at Otto, "Look at that broken-down hunk of tin. What a loser. Where're ya goin', loser? Afraid of A Clifford? Look at the chicken."

Fullsom was still flapping his arms and making idiotic chicken noises when the starting flag went down. All the other cars whizzed by, leaving him in the dust.

CHAPTER 2

A Quick Change

Otto stopped at the pit and picked up The Aunts. He drove Racecar to a deserted area.

"Did you see the message?" asked Otto.

"I certainly did," said Aunt FooFoo. "It's a disaster. A Clifford won the race while you were playing games with that chicken guy."

18

"And you broke the car too," said Aunt FiFi, "just when I had it in tip-top shape."

"Racecar is fine," said Otto. "I just needed an excuse to leave the track. That writing was a message for us. We have to get to Cliff Road now. We're on a mission."

"We are?" asked FiFi.

"Why didn't you say so?" said FooFoo. "We have to change. Where's the phone booth?"

"There is no phone booth. Just change right here. There's no one around."

"That stinks," said FooFoo, pouting. "Superman always got to change in a phone booth."

Otto brought their disguises out from a secret compartment under the backseat.

They changed into . . .

The Uncles

CHAPTER 4

Otto aka Otto

It's a fact that most grown-ups and all bad guys have a genetic defect that prevents them from telling one kid from another, even if the kid is a famous racecar driver. Otto didn't need a disguise.

Racecar

But everyone recognized Racecar.

Otto pulled one of his shoelaces. A computer screen shot out from the toe of his shoe. He pressed the end of the shoelace to where the screen said *Option Five*.

Racecar's trunk opened up, and an *electronic arm* came out holding a can of tuna.

The can actually contained Racecar's Morphing Formula. The arm dumped the contents onto Racecar. A dense liquid spread over the car and turned into a jelly that bubbled and hardened. In moments Racecar was completely hidden inside the shell of a truck. Letters on the side said:

**Top Spot Mobile Shoe Shine
Friman and Froman Brothers,
Proprietors**

On the roof was a revolving foot.

TOP
SPOT
MOBILE SHOE
SHINE
———•———
FRIMAN
&
FROMAN
BROTHERS
PROPRIETORS

CHAPTER 6

A Discovery

Sixteen minutes later they arrived at Cliff Road.

They got out of the truck and found themselves on a deserted bluff overlooking the ocean.

"Okay," said FiFi. "This is it. Looks like we're going to have to scout it out down below. FooFoo, jump."

FooFoo started to take a running leap when Otto shouted, "Stop!"

"Okeydoke," said FooFoo.

"Get back in the car," he said urgently. "We might have to get out of here fast. The tide is too low, and the water is rushing backward. These are perfect conditions for a tidal wave."

"Windshield magnifier," he said to Racecar. "Let's see what the **outlook** is over this **lookout**."

Powerful magnifying glass replaced the normal glass in Racecar's front window. They all looked.

Stunned, they saw a whirlpool funnel spinning way out in the ocean, sucking the water into it.

"It's not a tidal wave," said Otto.

"Thank goodness," said Aunt FooFoo.

"It's way worse. There must be some kind of hole at the bottom of that whirlpool," he gulped, "because this sea is *sinking*!!!!!"

An Exclamation

"Nooooo!!!"

screamed The Aunts.

CHAPTER 8

Dried Fruit

"Yeeesss!!!" screamed Otto back.

"Here," he said, taking out three tiny brown dots and three small red dots.

"The brown dots are interactive global positioning transmitters, or GPSs for short. I designed them to look like freckles, and here are the receivers. They look like pimples. They're hooked up to Racecar's dashboard computer. We'll all wear them, so if we're ever separated, the people who are with Racecar will be able to locate the ones who aren't. If there's ever an emergency, speak into your freckle and say, *'Derek, I like red.'* That'll be our code. Got it? Put them on."

Otto and FiFi put theirs on their arms. FooFoo put her freckle on her

Derek, I like red is a palindrome.

28

nostril, and her pimple on the tip of her nose.

Just then, they saw a figure running toward them, up the sand dunes and the rocks. They all got out of Racecar just as the runner reached the top of the cliff. It was a teenage boy, and he was frantic.

He grabbed on to Aunt FiFi.

"I am not Raisin Boy!" he gasped desperately. He tore off his T-shirt, which said *Raisin Boy*.

Then he saw Otto. "Oh look, just your size." He slipped the T-shirt over Otto's head, took one quick look behind him, and ran off wildly, shouting, "Free the snakes, free the lizards."

CHAPTER 9

More Dried Fruit

When Otto turned around, he was face-to-face with the ugliest man he had ever seen. His skin was shriveled up and the color of worms. His lips were black, and the whites of his eyes were gray. He had two teeth. They were rotten. He was wearing a T-shirt that said *Prune Man*. It was easy to see why.

CHAPTER 10

Foot Shine

Prune Man tapped Otto on the shoulder.

"Tag. You're it," he said in a voice that was like gravel.

"I am?" said Otto.

"You are if I said so, aren't you? I'm the Prune and you're the Raisin," sneered Prune Man.

Prune Man couldn't tell the difference between Otto and the boy he had been chasing, even though they didn't look anything alike and they weren't even the same age. Prune Man had *bad guy* written all over him.

"Shoe shine?" said FiFi, coming over with a shoe-shine kit.

"Have a seat," said FooFoo, coming over with a chair.

"Who are these guys?" asked Prune Man suspiciously.

"Friman and Froman Brothers Mobile Shoe Shine. FriFri Friman, general manager," said FriFri, introducing herself.

"Why do you always get to be the general?" asked FooFoo.

"Zip it," said FiFi. "We have a special. Two shoes for the price of one, only $1.25."

"These aren't my shoes, they're my feet. Strong as leather. Smell nice too." Prune Man stuck his foot in FiFi's face.

It was so stinky, she fell down.

"Okay, shine 'em up," said Prune Man. Prune Man sat down. FiFi held her nose with one hand, and with the other started applying black shoe polish to

his feet with a rag.

"Ooo, oo, ticklish," said Prune Man. He started laughing hysterically in his painfully scratchy voice. "Okay, shine's over. After tag comes piggyback."

He picked Otto up, put him on his shoulders, and ran back down the steep hill.

"Be home in time for dinner," called Aunt FooFoo.

"Where are you going, you big piece of beef jerky?" yelled FiFi. "You owe us $1.25 for shining your smelly old feet."

"Bad guys, these days," sighed FooFoo, putting her arm around her sister. "You just can't trust them."

33

CHAPTER 11

The Hideout

Prune Man dumped Otto onto the sand, then whistled loudly.

A camel came galloping down the beach toward them. "Whoa Winkie," said Prune Man. The camel stopped and bent down. "Up, up, up," said Prune Man to Otto. They both got on, and Winkie took off.

As they rode down the beach, Otto saw what looked like an enormous mountain looming in front of them.

But it wasn't a mountain. It was a giant, rippling blob. The blob was knotted on top and attached by a rope to a rocket on a launch pad. The bottom was wrapped around a vacuum cleaner hose that ran along the sand toward the ocean.

Winkie stopped at a hut. There was a sign on it that said **CONTAMINATED— NO ADMITTANCE**. Prune Man shoved Otto through the door.

In the middle of the room was a control board, labeled *Aqua-Vac*. A single lever jutted out from the board, regulating three speeds: *On–Regular*, *On–Maximum the Most*, and *Off*. The lever now pointed to *On–Regular*.

Otto noticed a tube reading out a water level. It was less than half full. It took him only a few seconds to put it all together. The Aqua-Vac was sucking the ocean's water into the blob outside, which was actually a giant water balloon.

Otto was too close to Prune Man to talk into his freckle. All he could do was tap out an *SOS* and hope The Aunts would get the message.

Contaminated is an anagram for no admittance.
SOS is a palindrome. It means HELP!

36

CHAPTER 12

Back at the Cliff, Part 1

FiFi's and FooFoo's pimple receivers were giving off a signal.

"Hey, my arm is beeping," said FiFi.

"My nose is beeping," said FooFoo.

"That's annoying," said FiFi.

They turned them off.

Chow Time

"What do you say, I whip us up some chow?" said Prune Man. "Since it's your last meal, I'll take requests."

"Last meal?" gulped Otto.

"Yahoo hay!" said Prune Man. Without waiting for Otto's answer, Prune Man got out some bread and made two hay sandwiches. He gave one to Otto.

"Uh, thanks," said Otto. "Could I please have something to drink?"

"Sure enough," said Prune Man. He poured Otto a large glass of flour.

"I mean something wet," said Otto.

Prune Man laughed and gave Otto some head noogies. "What a crack-up," he said.

Eleven plus two is an anagram for twelve plus one.
Yahoo hay is a palindrome.

38

There's someone in this room who's a little more cracked up than I am, thought Otto.

"Hey, wait a minute," said Prune Man. "You haven't been sneaking water, have you?"

"Who, me?" asked Otto. He wasn't too sure what the right answer was.

"That's extremely disappointing, Raisin Boy," said Prune Man roughly.

"You know that you and I get all the moisture we need through our ears, and that water is poison to us."

"Oh sure, I know that," said Otto, feeling worse about things every second.

"When we blast all the oceans into outer space, we'll be the only ones who are able to survive besides these guys," said Prune Man.

Otto looked around. Against the walls were cages filled with desert animals. They looked pretty dried out, even for lizards and snakes and tortoises. A few of them had their tongues hanging out.

"You know something, you're not acting right at all," said Prune Man suspiciously. "Come to think of it, you look small and weeny, not at all the way you used to look."

"Uhm, that's because it's the weekend," said Otto, "and a lot of my big bones are resting." *Boy, was that dumb,* he thought to himself. He held his breath, hoping that Prune Man didn't figure out he wasn't the real Raisin Boy.

"Oh yeah," said Prune Man.

Whew, thought Otto. Now if his aunts would only respond to his call.

CHAPTER 14

Back at the Cliff, Part 2

FooFoo and FiFi were taking turns shining each other's shoes.

"I wish Otto would come back," said FooFoo. "I miss him."

"Children can be very ungrateful," said FiFi. "You feed them, give them a roof over their heads, change their tires and spark plugs, and then they go and leave you for a large prune guy. Sheesh!"

"Leave them alone and they'll come home, wagging their tails behind them," said FooFoo.

"That's sheep," said FiFi.

"What is?" asked FooFoo.

"The ones who come home with the tails," said FiFi.

"Who said?" asked FooFoo.

"That Bo Peep girl," said FiFi.

"What does she know?" asked FooFoo.

"Exactly," said FiFi.

"She never even met Otto," said FooFoo. "What nerve."

"Let's eat," said FiFi.

"Now you're talking. I made a scrumptious lunch," said FooFoo.

She opened the shoe-shine box and took out two sea-bass-and-Limburger-cheese sandwiches with pumpkin chili, on chocolate-cake bread.

"Mmm," said FiFi without much enthusiasm.

They took their food into the shoe-car and turned on the *satellite TV*, which was hooked up to Racecar's dashboard computer.

CHAPTER 15

Hail, the Emperor

Prune Man was happily munching his second hay sandwich.

"Don't forget our motto," he said. "Like the tortoise, eat a leaf. No water for a year, and also no beef. Also **no lemons, no melon**."

"Excuse me, Master Prune," said Otto.

"James T. Justerson, Emperor!" said Prune Man indignantly.

"Excuse me, Emperor," said Otto.

"Sure, what did you do, burp?" asked Prune Man.

"No, I mean I have something to say," said Otto.

"Well, spit it out," said Prune Man.

Spit was actually something Otto had very little of at the moment.

No lemons, no melon is a palindrome.

44

"Even if the oceans dry up, people will have water to drink," he said, "because they drink the fresh water from reservoirs, not the salty water from the oceans."

"Says you," said Prune Man.

"Really," said Otto. "The problem is that if the oceans dry up, all the animals and plants in the sea will die, and then it'll stop raining and all the other plants on Earth will die, and then there won't be any oxygen in the atmosphere, so all the animals and people won't be able to breathe."

"Says you," said Prune Man.

"Even if you and me and all the desert animals can live with hardly any water," continued Otto, "we're going to die too, because we can't live without air. We still need to breathe."

"Look, smarty-pants Raisin *boob*," said Prune Man. "I'm going to hold all the world's ocean water ransom in outer

Boob is a palindrome.

space. If people want it back, which they will, they're going to have to pay for it, by the dropful. And it won't be cheap. When I have all that money, I'll be too rich to breathe."

Otto tapped his freckle frantically.

CHAPTER 16

Back at the Cliff, Part 3

The Aunts were flicking through the channels on Racecar's TV.

"What is this station?" said FiFi. "It looks like a dancing freckle or something."

"That's a terrible dance," said FooFoo. "I'm sure they can find more talented freckles to put on TV."

Just then, her nose pimple itched, so she scratched it. It started beeping.

"Look," said FooFoo. "That no-talent freckle is dancing in time to my beeping pimple."

"Wait a minute," said FiFi.

CHAPTER 17

Back at the Cliff, Part 3¹/₄

FooFoo waited.

CHAPTER 18

Back at the Cliff, Part 3½

"That's not a no-talent freckle," said FiFi a minute later. "That's Otto."

"Why is he dancing around like that?" asked FooFoo. "What a goofball."

"Actually," said FiFi, "I believe his dancing is a twisted cry for help. Otto may be in trouble."

"Oh no," gasped Aunt FooFoo. "We have to find him." FooFoo rushed out of the car and jumped off the cliff.

"Wait a minute," yelled Aunt FiFi.

"You forgot the car."

"Wait a minute," she yelled again. "You forgot me!" Then, noticing that she was the only one left, FiFi sprang into action.

She dialed up Options on the dashboard computer and chose number 2. Racecar shed the shoe covering, and morphed into his *Mission Disguise*.

She flipped the *Dune Buggy* switch. The regular tires folded up, and large ones took their place. FiFi drove Racecar off the cliff and down the sandy mountain.

CHAPTER 19

Chip off the Old Ice Block

"It's time for your final test," said Prune Man.

He gave Otto a piece of paper. On it were four multiple-choice questions.

"What do I get if I get everything right?" asked Otto.

"A ride in a rocket," said Prune Man.

"What do I get if I get everything wrong?" asked Otto.

"A ride in a rocket," said Prune Man.

Otto looked at the paper.

1. At 1300 hours you make your way to the launch _____.
   a. puppy
   b. poopy

c. grandma

d. pad

Otto chose *d. pad.*

2. At 1308 you say good-bye to the _____.

    a. puppy

    b. poopy

    c. grandma

    d. world

Otto chose *d. world.*

3. At 1315 you enter the rocket _____.

    a. puppy

    b. poopy

    c. grandma

    d. ship

Otto sighed and chose *d. ship.*

4. At 1316 you blast off into outer _____.

    a. puppy

    b. poopy

    c. grandma

    d. space

Otto knew it was wrong, but he couldn't help it. He ignored all the choices and wrote in *e. your mind.*

He handed back his paper.

Prune Man quickly marked the answers.

"You got everything correct, except number 4. The right answer was *d. space.* You blast off into outer space," he said. "Where in the world is 'outer your mind' anyway? Let's see, there were four questions, equaling 100 percent. Each question was worth 25 percent, and you got three of them right, which gives you a total score of 75 percent. Congratulations. You are only 25 percent stupid."

He dug his hand into a sack and pulled out a space suit and a helmet. "Put these on," he demanded. "There's a rocket out there with your name on it."

Still not sure how he fit into Prune Man's plan, Otto bowed humbly and asked, "Emperor, when I'm up in outer space, what am I supposed to do?"

"Look, Raisin idiot, we've gone over this a hundred times. You're starting to get on my nerves. You know there are plenty of other dry boys out there who would pay me to do your job," he threatened.

"Oh no," said Otto, "I just want to be 100 percent sure. You can't be too careful when flying around in outer space, you know."

"Okay, for the last time, you get blasted into outer space with the balloon full of ocean water. The water freezes into a ball of ice about the size of the moon. Every time you get a trans-mission from me, you take a little space walk, chip off a piece of ice, put it in one of the millions of

GOOD
EMPEROR
PRUNES
WET
WATER
DRINK

bottles I've supplied labeled *Good Emperor Prune's Wet Water Drink*, and send it back to me on Earth in a minirocket. Other than that, you can spend your days for the next 20 years coloring. I've provided crayons and paper."

"Oh yes, now I remember," lied Otto. "I'll just be a minute changing into my space suit."

Otto went into a corner of the hut to change. He was finally in a place private enough to speak into his freckle.

CHAPTER 20

Talking Zits

FiFi glanced at the TV screen as she drove down the beach. The freckle was jumping again, and a scratchy voice was coming from her pimple.

"*IrfIrf, OrfOrf*, come in, come in," said Otto.

FiFi spoke into her freckle. "Who is it?" she asked suspiciously.

"*Derek, I like red,*" said Otto.

"I don't know any Derek," said FiFi.

The plan was breaking down. Otto didn't have time for any more delays. "It's me, Otto," he said.

"How do I know you're not a Tasmanian spy?" asked FiFi.

"*FriFri, daer eht SPG. Yrruh!*" said Otto.

"*Tog ti,*" said FiFi, finally convinced by their backward code.

"*Em oot, em oot,*" FooFoo's voice came over the pimple.

A second later FiFi saw her sister bounding down the sand in front of her. She pressed a button, swinging open Racecar's door, and FooFoo jumped in. They sped off to the hut at 200 mph.

"*FriFri, daer eht SPG. Yrruh!*" is backward for "IrfIrf, read the GPS. Hurry!"
Tog ti is backward for Got it.
Em oot, em oot is backward for Me too, me too.

CHAPTER 21

Quick Switch

Prune Man pushed the lever on the Aqua-Vac control board up to *On–Maximum the Most*. "Let's go," he said.

In the secret-agent business, sometimes you just have to get lucky, and this time Otto did.

The Aunts arrived at the hut just as a flash sandstorm kicked up.

Prune Man opened the door. FiFi was standing right there, but he couldn't see her. She couldn't see him, either.

"Lousy weather," said Prune Man. "We'll take the camel."

Luckily, Otto had installed a *night-vision flashlight* on his *radar-tracking ring*. He flicked it on for a

58

moment. He saw his aunt in front of him, and Racecar right behind her.

Prune Man, screaming for Winkie, was paying no attention to Otto.

Otto whispered, "*IrfIrf*, I have a plan."

"Where are you?" she asked.

"I'm right next to you," he said. "You can touch me."

"Hey, you don't feel like Otto at all," said FiFi, reaching out her hand. "You feel

all squishy, like a Tasmanian spy!"

Otto heard Winkie galloping toward them.

"*Pots, IrfIrf*, I'm wearing a space suit, but I want you to put it on," he said, taking off the suit. "Go with Prune Man and pretend to be me, and whatever you do, keep the helmet on and don't get into any rocket ships. I'll be back as soon as I can."

"Say, 'Please, wise General,'" said FiFi.

"Please, wise General," sighed Otto.

FiFi put on the spacesuit.

All of a sudden FiFi felt a pair of hands clamp down on her shoulders.

"There you are, Astro Raisin Boy," said Prune Man. "Up, up, up!" He ushered her onto Winkie and rode off into the sand.

CHAPTER 22

One Aunt

As soon as they were gone, Otto jumped into Racecar, put up the *night-vision windshield* and *sand blower*, and took off toward the ocean.

"Hey," said Aunt FooFoo, "you're not my sister."

"No," said Otto, "I'm your nephew. Your sister is stalling Prune Man so we

can deactivate the Aqua-Vac."

"Swell," said FooFoo. She had no idea what Otto was talking about.

"The Aqua-Vac is sucking all the water in the ocean into a big water balloon," he explained.

"If it's a water balloon, why don't we just pop it?" she asked.

"Because if we do that, or even switch it off suddenly, the rush of ocean water would make tidal waves that could cause chain reactions of catastrophic damage all

over the world," said Otto.

"Oh," said FooFoo. "Then let's go home."

"No," said Otto. "We're going to have to clamp off the Aqua-Vac hose, which is probably at the bottom of the whirlpool on the ocean floor. Then we have to release the water, little by little, letting it run back into the sea gradually."

"You're pretty smart, aren't you?" said FooFoo.

"I guess," said Otto.

"You look kind of dopey as a freckle though," said FooFoo.

"Uh-huh," said Otto.

"And be sure to take some dance lessons before you appear on any other television shows," she added.

CHAPTER 23

Scuba Dooba Doo

Otto and FooFoo raced toward the water. The tide was so far out that a few small boats and a *kayak* lay stranded on the beach.

Suddenly a scuba diver stepped right out in front of them. Otto hit the brakes

Kayak is a palindrome.

and swerved to miss him, but the diver fell down anyway.

"Are you all right, sir?" asked Otto.

"Tip-top," said the diver, "but, I say, have you seen the water? It seems to be missing."

"It's about a mile or two out that way," said Otto, pointing.

"Would you be kind enough to give an old chap a lift?" asked the diver. "These flippers are a bit hard on the ankles."

He was an older and very dapper English gentleman with a rather wide butt.

"Hop in," said Otto, who thought that it was a stroke of luck that they had him. A dive directly into the whirlpool funnel might be their only hope of getting to the source of the vacuum hose.

"We could use your diving skills to help save the world," said Otto.

"Smashing," said the diver. "A good

adventure dive is exactly what I'm looking for. I used to dive for Sir James Bond while I was employed by Her Majesty's Secret Service, you know. Does it involve sunken treasure at all, *pip pip*?"

"Sir, I believe James Bond is a fictional character," said Otto.

"Quite right, aren't we all," said the diver merrily.

CHAPTER 24

CarBoat CarBoat CarBoat CarBoat CarBoat CarBoat

"I say, old chaps, lovely vehicle, absolutely grand," said the diver, squeezing into the backseat.

They had reached the ocean. "Buckle up," said Otto. "We're going into *Hover Mode*." Otto had recently equipped

Racecar with this new upgrade.

He flipped a switch on the dashboard. Racecar's wheels folded up, and the bottom of the car became an air chamber.

"Uncle OrfOrf, start the *pump*," said Otto.

A handle came up from underneath the passenger seat. FooFoo pumped it a few times to get the pressure going, and then put it on automatic. Racecar now had full hovercraft capabilities.

"Oh, great fun," said the diver. "Did you

say your name was Orf?" he asked FooFoo.

"Why yes," she said sweetly. FooFoo liked the diver.

"I knew an Orf back in jolly old. A Donald Orf. Any relation?" he asked.

"Jolly old what?" asked FooFoo.

The diver burst out laughing. "England, old chap, jolly old England. What a cutup! Just like old Orfy. We'll have to have a spot of tea, and catch up on old times."

"Oh yes," said FooFoo. "Are you *married*, by any chance?" She was quite an *admirer*.

"Whirlpool ahead," interrupted Otto, just in time.

Married is an anagram for admirer.

CHAPTER 25

Tug-of-Helmet

Prune Man and FiFi hadn't gotten very far at all when Winkie, not being able to see where she was going, smashed head-on into the water balloon. They both fell off. The sandstorm suddenly stopped raging.

Prune Man got his bearings, stepped on Winkie's hoof, and pinched her in the hump. "Stupid camel. Can't even find her way in a little sand."

That made Winkie plenty angry. She spit a wad of camel saliva in Prune Man's face and ran off down the beach.

"Who cares about you, Winkie," yelled Prune Man. "When I'm emperor of the world I'll have 900 camels and you won't even be one of them."

Prune Man and FiFi were trudging along in the sand. FiFi kept tugging on the space suit, which was hanging down around her ankles.

"Say, Raisin Boy, you should have eaten that other hay sandwich," said

Prune Man. "You're looking a little puny."

FiFi nodded in agreement.

"Take off your helmet so we can go over final details," said Prune Man.

FiFi shook her head no.

Prune Man pulled the helmet. FiFi yanked it back. They tumbled onto the sand, tugging the helmet and rolling around, until they both realized they had rolled right in front of the rocket.

Prune Man let go, pumped his arm in the air, and said, "Yes!"

FiFi put her hand inside her space suit and squeezed her freckle.

CHAPTER 26

Fashion Show

Otto's pimple was beeping. FiFi needed him. He had to get the job done quickly.

The hovercar was in position just over the whirlpool, which spun faster and faster as the oceans were being sucked up.

"All right, sir, here's the plan," said Otto to the diver. "We attach this line to your waist, and you dive into the eye of the whirlpool. On the bottom of the sea you'll find a vacuum hose. Just pick it up and bring it back to the surface."

Otto attached one end of the rope to Racecar's steering column.

"Righto," said the diver, "Lovely. I say, how deep are these waters?"

"Deep," said Otto, checking the Hover-Racecar's *underwater periscope*. "Approximately 231 feet, $9^1/_{16}$ inches."

"Quite," said the diver. "Sorry, lad, I never go in over my head."

Otto was stunned. "Why do you have all that equipment then?" he asked.

"Because I look absolutely smashing in it, of course. Don't you think?" asked the diver.

"Oh yes, so smashing," said FooFoo.

This was going nowhere. Otto attached the rope to himself.

"Would you mind if I borrowed your suit and tank and stuff?" he asked. "I'm going to have to do this dive myself."

"Jolly good, lad," said the diver. "I'll exchange the whole lot of it for that Raisin Boy T-shirt. High style, I say. It's smashing!"

Otto put on the scuba gear. The diver put on the T-shirt.

"Oh fab," he said joyfully.

"So fab," said FooFoo, practically swooning.

Otto did not know how to swim. He was afraid of deep water. He heard the voices of his parents in his head, echoing what they had said to him in their last letter: *"learn to swim. . . . secret agents often get thrown into the deep end of the pool.*" It didn't get any deeper than this.

Otto looked into the dark, swirling water. He took a long breath. He swallowed hard. He put the breathing tube in his mouth. He couldn't move.

"I say, lad, the best way to get over your fear of something is to dive right into it," said the diver. "That's what we do back in jolly old." And the diver put out his arm and pushed Otto over the side.

CHAPTER 27

It

Otto was sucked down into the whirlpool. It turned him around in circles like a corkscrew. It took him down fast, and with an intense force. Then he saw it.

The mouth of the vacuum hose was 50 feet away. But this was not an ordinary hose. It was 3 feet wide, and he was heading straight for it.

What was he going to use to plug it up? Hopefully not himself!

He only had a split second and four chapters to figure it out.

CHAPTER 28

The Countdown

There was a long set of stairs leading up to the door of the rocket. Prune Man was at the controls.

"Okay, Raisin kiddie, all systems are go. Smile." Prune Man put his arm around FiFi. He took out a camera and snapped a picture. Then he flipped a switch.

"T minus 5 minutes," beamed an automated voice from the launch control.

"Begin your historic climb," said Prune Man dramatically.

FiFi didn't move.

"Begin your historic climb!" he said again.

She had to stall for time. "Wait a second," she mumbled.

Stalling for Time

"Why?" asked Prune Man.

More Stalling for Time

"Because," said FiFi.

Enough Stalling for Time

"Because why?" asked Prune Man.

"I have an itch on my back and I can't reach it," FiFi said suddenly, and she started jumping around and scratching like a maniac.

"Don't just stand there," she cried. "Help me."

She hopped from one foot to the other, yelling out back-scratching directions.

"A little to the left, no, a little to the  right, higher, you almost had it, lower, lower, over to the side, a little more, that's it, that's it, no, no, over to the—"

There was a beep

from the launch-control module. "T minus 4 minutes and 30 seconds," said the voice.

"That's it," said Prune Man, "No more scratching. You're going up NOW!"

FiFi needed another idea.

Bingo!

She started up the stairs to the rocket. Three steps up she broke into a tap dance. She tapped her way up five steps, and shuffled down three, tapped up four, shuffled down seven. She did some turns, she did some jumps. She was dazzling.

Prune Man stood there with his mouth open. Then the voice said, "T minus 4 minutes."

CHAPTER 32

Back to Otto

It was a split second and four chapters later, and Otto still didn't have an idea.

Desperate, he was about to throw himself across the vacuum mouth when a huge stingray brushed against him. It was five feet wide and completely white. Otto thought he was dreaming.

Otto had a strong belief in the intelligence of animals, and this one was purposefully going straight toward the vacuum. The albino stingray looked at Otto as he passed.

Otto understood.

Without touching the spiny poisonous tail, he stretched out his arms as wide as he could and grabbed on to the

stingray's wings. He guided it to the
mouth of the hose.

The stingray was perfect, like a giant
rubber stopper in a bathroom drain. It
wasn't hurt either. The whirlpool stopped.

Otto wanted to shout, he was so happy,
but luckily he remembered that opening
your mouth underwater is a no-no. Instead

he did the twist, his favorite dance for all happy occasions. Then he jumped onto the vacuum hose, wrapped his legs around it, and paddled upward.

Everything seemed to be going well for about 15 seconds.

Then he ran out of air.

CHAPTER 33

What the Other Guys Were Doing

Prune Man ran up the stairs after FiFi.

"Look, I'm really sick of you, little chicken Raisin baby, afraid of a teeny weeny rocket ride." He tried to grab her. She hung off the railing. He tried to grab her again. She swung around to the other side.

The voice said, "T minus 3 minutes and 30 seconds."

Prune Man aimed carefully and pounced.

He got his hands around her ankles, and dragged her up the stairs to the rocket door.

CHAPTER 34

More Otto

Otto couldn't believe he had been so dumb. He hadn't even checked the air gauge on the tank. He did now, and it read *empty*. He had no choice but to hold his breath and make it to the top as quickly as possible.

It was a good thing that he and The Aunts had a weekly breath-holding contest, which he always won. He was up to $2\frac{1}{2}$ minutes. But was that long enough to get to the top?

He paddled up in fast motion.

Just as he thought his lungs were going to explode, he broke through the surface of the water to the air.

Then he remembered something.

CHAPTER 35

Something

He still couldn't swim.

Otto gasped, took a deep breath, and immediately went under again.

Flash

Prune Man was about to unlock the door to the rocket when FiFi started weeping.

"Stop that," said Prune Man.

"I don't want to go," she bawled, holding on to him. "I'm going to miss you so much when I'm in outer space."

"I understand, little Raisin lump. Twenty years is a long time not to see me," he said, patting her on the helmet.

"Can I at least have a picture of you to take with me?" she sniffed.

"Oh, okay," said Prune Man.

He handed her the camera and leaned against the rocket, smiling widely, showing his two rotten teeth.

FiFi put the camera right up to his face and snapped the picture.

"Auggghhh!" he screamed, blinded by the flash.

FiFi started down the stairs.

It was T minus 60 seconds.

CHAPTER 37

Splash

FooFoo was sitting on the pontoon of the hovercar, feeling a little seasick. The diver was trying to help her with a series of breathing instructions.

"Deep breaths, old chap, head between the knees, arms overhead, feet higher than the heart, toes to the nose, chin up, do the Hokey Pokey and turn yourself around, that's what it's all about."

That's when Otto surfaced on the vacuum hose and then quickly disappeared.

"Did you hear a splash?" asked FooFoo.

"I say, old chap, something rose out of the ocean. It looked like a stingray on a pipe with a small boy on top," said the diver.

"Uh-huh," said FooFoo.

"The young man looked familiar, actually. Can't quite place him though," said the diver.

"I don't care about him," said FooFoo. "I just wish Otto would come back already."

"That's it. Well done, man. That's who it is. The young lad who went off with my equipment," said the diver.

FooFoo, her mind suddenly clear as a bell, jumped into the ocean to rescue Otto.

CHAPTER 38

Noble Ray

Otto, not one to wait for a rescue party, pulled himself out of the water by the rope attached to his waist.

When he surfaced, FooFoo grabbed him around the neck in a lifesaving move.

"Don't worry, I've got you." She was crying her eyes out. "I'm so so so sorry I let you go into the water, Ottie. I was blinded by mad crazy love."

Otto held fast to the vacuum hose so it wouldn't sink back into the ocean. He couldn't talk because FooFoo was holding his neck so tightly she was almost choking him.

"Give him mouth-to-mouth, quickly," yelled FooFoo. "He's been under too long. He's losing power to his brain. His

94

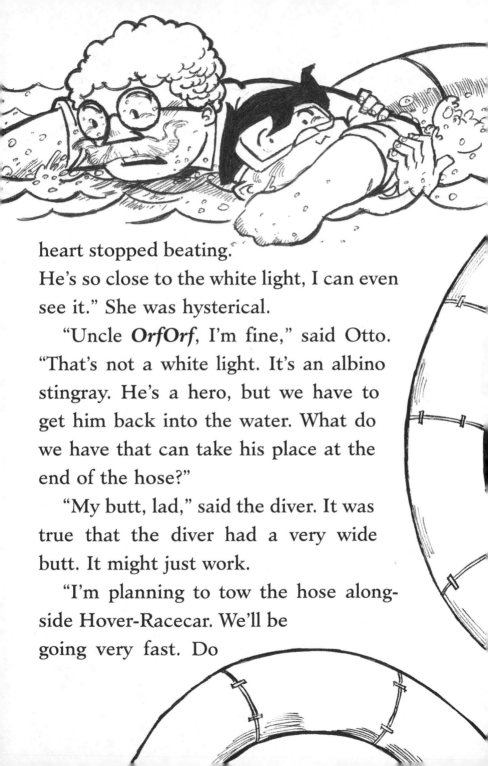

heart stopped beating.
He's so close to the white light, I can even
see it." She was hysterical.

"Uncle *OrfOrf*, I'm fine," said Otto.
"That's not a white light. It's an albino
stingray. He's a hero, but we have to
get him back into the water. What do
we have that can take his place at the
end of the hose?"

"My butt, lad," said the diver. It was
true that the diver had a very wide
butt. It might just work.

"I'm planning to tow the hose along-
side Hover-Racecar. We'll be
going very fast. Do

you think you'll be able to stay on?" asked Otto.

"Of course, dear boy. I'm fit as a fiddle. Start every day with 300 sit-ups and a pound of lard straight up," said the diver.

"Really?" said FooFoo. "Have you ever tried it roasted, with pickled popcorn? It's delish!"

"Okay," said Otto. "On the count of three, let's make the switch. One, two, three!"

Otto and FooFoo removed the stingray as the diver slid into place on the hose. Then Otto gently lowered the noble ray back into the ocean, thanked it silently, and watched it swim away.

Otto got into the driver's seat. FooFoo sat behind the diver on the vacuum hose.

"Just let me apply a dollop of my super hair gel, guaranteed to resist water and winds of up to 240 kilometers per hour," said the diver. "**A *gentleman*** must always be an ***elegant man***, you know."

Otto swung Racecar around and

A gentleman is an anagram for elegant man.

headed back to FiFi and the Aqua-Vac.

Seconds later a few drops of water fell from the sky.

"Hurry, Ottie. It's raining," yelled FooFoo.

Otto stuck out his hand and tasted the water. "No, it's not," he said. "That's seawater. That can only mean one thing. The balloon has sprung a leak!" He threw a couple of helmets to FooFoo and the diver. "Put these on. We have to move!"

He pushed the gears into *Hyperspeed Plus One*, and took off.

CHAPTER 39

Broken Helmet, Rushing Water

FiFi didn't get very far, going down the stairs. Prune Man caught her again three steps from the top.

It was T minus 40 seconds.

Water was squirting out from holes all over the balloon.

"I put some tape in the rocket,"

said Prune Man. "Pretty smart, huh? First thing you do when you get up there is take a refreshing space walk and patch that thing."

Now FiFi was frantic.

Prune Man pressed the door lock button. The door slid open.

Suddenly there was a screech of brakes, as Otto and Racecar came to a halt at the launch pad.

FiFi was so excited to hear it that she screamed her piercing scream in the note of A-flat. This turned out to be the best thing she could have done. Her helmet cracked apart from the sound, and Prune Man had to let her go to hold his ears.

It was T minus 30 seconds.

"Hold on tight," Otto said to the diver. "I'm going into the hut to shut down the Aqua-Vac. When I do, the water is going to flow the other way, out of the hose. You will feel extreme pressure, but you have to resist."

"Can do, lad. I'm highly trained, you know. In the old days I stood under Niagara Falls wearing nothing but a beanie. Best shower I ever had," said the diver.

Otto pressed a button on his belt, which released his newest invention for every-day sportswear, Motorized Kangaroo

Jumping Shoes. He hopped away.

"Hey, you're not Raisin Boy," said Prune Man to FiFi. "You and that other dude are those shoe-shine guys."

"That's right, you dehydrated nut job, and you still owe us $1.25," said FiFi.

The voice beamed, "T minus 20 seconds."

Suddenly there was a shout as the water reversed direction.

"Egad, men, *Niagara O roar again*!" wailed the diver.

Otto, back from the hut, leaped onto the hose and spoke into his remote control. *"Rear wheels up!"*

Racecar rose onto his front wheels. The hose was in the air, with Otto riding it and the diver on the end, aiming straight at Prune Man.

The voice said, "T minus 15 seconds."

"*Yo bozo boy*, get ready for your first bath!" shouted Otto.

Niagara O roar again is a palindrome.
Yo bozo boy is a palindrome.

"No! No water," screamed Prune Man, giving FiFi a final push.

FiFi lost her footing. She was falling into the rocket.

"Remove one butt cheek!" Otto yelled to the diver.

"Butt cheek off," said the diver. A strong stream of ocean water reached up to hit Prune Man directly in the face.

His skin turned into a mess of oozing, swelling hives. He started scratching and tearing at his cheeks.

Otto kept spraying.

Prune Man's entire body turned red, and blistery. He was writhing in agony and lost all control. He fell through the door, and into the rocket. FiFi pressed the door lock and ran down the stairs.

It was T minus 10 seconds.

Otto spoke into his remote.

"Wheels down!"

Racecar lowered his rear wheels. Otto jumped off the hose.

"We have to cut the rope connecting the balloon to the rocket," he said, "but we're out of time."

"I can do it, I'm the fastest," said FooFoo, which was true. She ran up the stairs.

It was T minus 7 seconds.

At the top of the stairs FooFoo grabbed the rope. She flipped out some scissors from her tool belt, and tried to cut it.

"It's too tough," she called. "FriFri, throw me your teeth!"

It was T minus 5 seconds.

FiFi took out her fierce false teeth and tossed them to her sister.

FooFoo caught them, put the rope between the teeth, and squeezed. The rope was cut. The balloon was free.

It was T minus 2 seconds. It was too late for FooFoo to get back down.

"Roof Catcher!" shouted Otto, positioning Racecar just under the stairs.

Racecar's roof softened into a cushy baseball glove.

"Jump!!" Otto yelled.

It was T minus 1 second.

FooFoo jumped, landing safely in the glove.

"We have liftoff," said the automated voice as the entire sky lit up, and the rocket shot into orbit in some galaxy—hopefully not ours.

Then Otto remembered the words of the original Raisin Boy. . . .

CHAPTER 40

The Words of the Original Raisin Boy

"Free the snakes, free the lizards."
"I'll be right back," said Otto.

CHAPTER 41

Freedom

Otto went into the hut and opened all the cages. He dumped out the containers of flour and hay, and filled them with water. The animals drank thankfully. He made sure to **step on no pets** and left the hut door open. He knew they'd all find their way home. His work here was done.

Step on no pets is a palindrome.

CHAPTER 42

Secrets Revealed

When Otto got back, the water balloon was completely empty.

"Remarkable adventure," said the diver. "Absolutely fab. Reminds me of the time

the Eboys and I defeated the dolphin *pirates* on a *sea trip* in the waters off Mozambique."

Otto was stunned.

"Did you say 'the Eboys and I'?" he asked.

"Did I?" asked the diver.

"Yes," said Otto.

"Blast, I don't think I was supposed to do that!" he exclaimed. "You Eboys are a tricky lot."

"So you must be an agent from *Eee YiiiY Eee*, and you know my parents," said Otto.

"Yes, they are my dear friends and colleagues in the agency," said the diver, "but please don't tell them I told you. They'd be rather miffed."

"Don't worry, I won't. I have no way to communicate with them, but please tell me, why do they have to be so secretive about everything? Why can't I ever see them?"

"You will, dear boy, as soon as they capture the tall skinny man with the enormous neck and the long dangling head. It's just taking a mite longer than they expected, about eight years so far."

Just then, a phone rang. The diver dug into a pocket in the side of his wet suit. He pulled a cell phone out of a plastic bag.

"**Rabbar** here," he answered.

Aha, thought Otto, noticing the palindrome. Then he noticed that *aha* was another palindrome.

"Oh dear, oh no, oh my, dear, dear, most unfortunate," said the diver into the phone. "I'll be there expresso-ly."

He hung up.

"Bad news?" asked Otto.

"Yes, I have to be off. I'm needed elsewhere, and so is my butt," he said. "Lovely to have met you all, let's do it again, shall we?"

Rabbar grabbed his scuba gear and loped off.

"I'm really a girl," shouted FooFoo.

But the diver didn't hear her. He had already disappeared down the beach.

CHAPTER 43

Gum and Chips

Straw Warts is a palindrome.
Nate's Hut is an anagram for The Aunts.
Toot is an anagram for Otto.

For the first time all day, Otto felt bad. There was so much he didn't know about his parents. All this secret-agency stuff was driving him crazy. If he was part of it, why did everything have to be a secret from him too?

Dejected, Otto gave the voice command *"Straw Warts"* to return Racecar back to his original shape, and drove up to the top of the cliff.

There, he was amazed to find a phone booth with a tag that said *Nate's Hut*, and a large gum ball machine with a tag that said **Toot**. They were gifts for Otto and The Aunts.

The Aunts were thrilled to be able to change back into their regular clothes in a phone booth, especially FooFoo.

Otto went over to the gum ball machine. He had loved these machines since he was a tiny boy. It was the kind that you put a quarter into, and get out a giant gum ball. Otto looked down and saw that there was already a quarter in the slot. All he had to do was turn the knob. He did. An orange gum ball came

out . . . his favorite.

He bit into it, and felt something hard and small inside. He dug it out of his mouth. It was a microchip. He returned to Racecar and inserted the chip into his handy *microchip reader*. The logo for ***Eee YiiiY Eee*** came up on the screen and then a very blurry image. It spoke.

"Hello, Jake. It's your father, Hogarth Eboy," said something blurry.

"Hello, darling boy. It's your mother,

too, Eleanor Eboy," said something else blurry.

"We're sorry if this image is difficult to see," continued a voice, "but, unfortunately, we were in the eye of a tornado when we recorded it.

"Word has reached us that you have completed your mission. We are so proud of you. You have brilliantly outsmarted one of the most evil people on the planet and saved the world from certain water balloon doom!

"We feel awful that we can't hug you at a moment like this, but you must never be seen with us, not until we capture the criminal Mr. *Rabbar* told you about. That evil man has sworn revenge on us. He does not know that you exist, and must not find out, for he would certainly try to hurt you.

"We hoped to be able to keep this from

you, as children should be able to play baseball and Candyland and not worry about getting killed all the time.

"Do you like the gum ball machine? Please chew only one gum ball at a time. When you were small, you stuffed eight of them into your mouth at once, and your jaw got stuck open for three hours.

"We'd love to hear you play the guitar sometime. If you stand on your amplifier while wearing an antenna hat, we may be able to pick up your frequency.

"For your own protection, please eat this microchip when you're finished with it. It's delicious with a glass of milk.

"'Bye for now. We love you *ytinifni reverof*."

The screen went blank.

For the first time ever, Otto let FiFi drive home. He had a lot to think about. He played his parents' message over and over. He had no memory of ever hearing their voices before. Even with the tornado in the background, he thought they were beautiful. When they got home, Otto poured himself a glass of milk and ate the microchip. It was the sweetest thing he had ever tasted.

Then he put on his antenna hat and went into the garage.

Singing the Blues

Otto popped another gum ball into his mouth. He didn't usually sing and chew gum at the same time, but this was a special occasion. He got out his guitar, put on his antenna hat, stood on his amplifier, and played the song that had been brewing in his head all day.

The Dried Fruit Blues
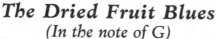

(In the note of G)

My ma-ma al - ways told me When I

was just a kid I could eat a prune

But that's nev - er what I did

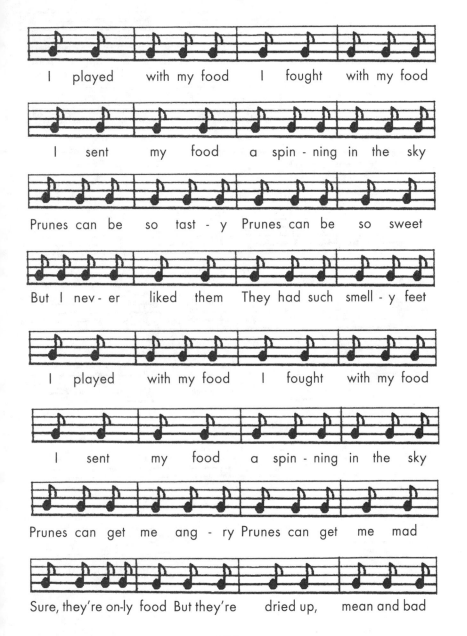

I played with my food I fought with my food

I sent my food a spin - ning in the sky

Prunes can be so tast - y Prunes can be so sweet

But I nev - er liked them They had such smell - y feet

I played with my food I fought with my food

I sent my food a spin - ning in the sky

Prunes can get me ang - ry Prunes can get me mad

Sure, they're on-ly food But they're dried up, mean and bad

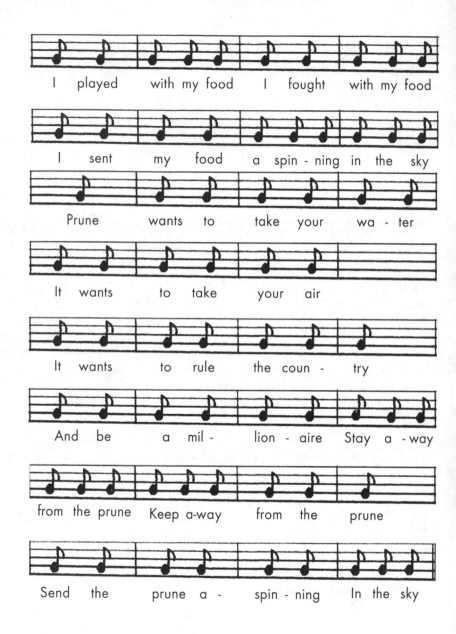

The End

Ha Ha, Fooled You

The real end.
The book is over.
Go home.
Get out of here.
Take a hike.
Do something else.

Stop reading!!!!!!

Crossword:
Water Balloon Doom

Across

1. Red dot used as a GPS receiver
2. *Pots* backward
5. Fastest car in the world
6. The Aunts' disguise
8. Winkie is his name
10. The bad guy's favorite food
11. Part of the name of this puzzle
13. The bad guy never played with a rubber duckie in one of these
15. A hero fish

Down

1. An anagram of *sea trip*
2. Outer _____
3. *Stop* backward
4. He wants to be emperor of the world
7. A "jolly old" country
9. It sits on a launchpad
11. The diver has a wide one
12. _____craft
14. Otto keeps his open for clues

Answers on page 128

Coming Soon!

Otto Undercover #4: Toxic Taffy Takeover

CHAPTER 1

Smoke and Bubbles

Otto's antenna hat started buzzing, the gum in his mouth started growing, his eye started pulsing, and he heard a rustling noise outside the garage window.

A giant bubble as big as his face popped out of his mouth. Wispy smoke swirled inside the bubble, creating letters that formed into an anagram—words with all their letters mixed up. It said:

Wiry neck toy

On tight

Then there was a loud crash as the garage window broke, and a long leg started feeling its way into the room.

CROSSWORD SOLUTION

DO NOT READ THIS PAGE!!!

Until You Do the Puzzle on
Page 126

By Order of the:

commission of CROSSWORD CRAZIES

Answer Key

BOCA RATON PUBLIC LIBRARY, FLORIDA

3 3656 0460188 0

J
Perlman, Rhea.
Water balloon doom /